Master Salt the Sailor's Son

By Allan Ahlberg
Illustrated by André Amstutz

GOLDEN PRESS • NEW YORK
Western Publishing Company, Inc.
Racine, Wisconsin

First published in the United Kingdom by Puffin Books/Kestrel Books.
Published in the U.S.A. in 1982.

Library of Congress Catalog Card Number: 81-84176
ISBN 0-307-31708-0 / ISBN 0-307-61708-4 (lib. bdg.)
A B C D E F G H I J

Mr. Salt the sailor sailed the seven seas.

Mrs. Salt sailed the seven seas, too.

So did Miss Salt.

Master Salt did not sail the seas.

He was too little.

He stayed on shore with his grandpa.

One day exciting things happened.
Mr. and Mrs. Salt got ready for a voyage.
  "We are going to sail
to Coconut Island," they said.

Mr. Salt cleaned the ship's cabins
and washed the deck.
Mrs. Salt and Sally Salt painted the funnel.
Sammy Salt sulked.
He wanted to go on a voyage, too.

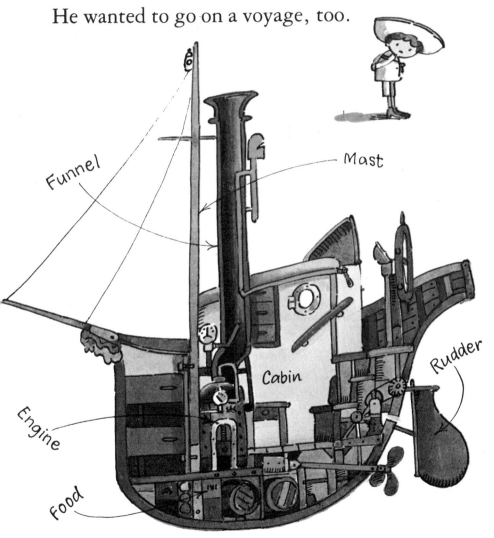

Funnel

Mast

Cabin

Rudder

Engine

Food

The next day the *Jolly Jack*
was ready to sail.
Mr. and Mrs. Salt pulled up the anchor.
Grandpa Salt stood on the shore.
But where was Sammy Salt?

The *Jolly Jack* sailed out to sea.
Sally Salt blew a kiss to her grandpa.
He waved good-bye from the shore.
But *where* was Sammy Salt?

The *Jolly Jack* sailed past a lighthouse.
Sally Salt got lunch ready.
Somebody's little hand reached out.
  "Who's been eating my fish?" asked Mr. Salt.

The *Jolly Jack* sailed past
a big ship.

Mr. Salt got a snack ready.
Somebody's little hand reached out again.
"Who's been eating *my* boiled egg?"
asked Mrs. Salt.

The *Jolly Jack* sailed past a whale.
Mrs. Salt got supper ready.
Somebody's little hand reached out again!
"Who's been drinking *my* cocoa?"
asked Sally Salt.

During the night strange things happened.
Sally Salt woke up.
She said her nose kept tickling.
"Don't be silly, Sally," said Mr. Salt.
Then Mr. Salt went to bed and *he* woke up.
"My nose keeps tickling," he said.

In the morning more strange things happened.
Somebody's little footprints appeared on deck.
Somebody's little teeth marks
appeared in an apple.
When Mr. Salt was fishing,
somebody's little boot appeared
on the end of his line.

Then, in the afternoon,
terrible things happened.
There was a storm.
The rain fell and the wind blew.
The thunder thundered and
the lightning flashed.
The *Jolly Jack* tipped up and down—
and Mr. Salt fell overboard!

"Man overboard!" shouted Mr. Salt.

Mrs. Salt came to the rescue.
But still the *Jolly Jack* tipped up
and down—and Mrs. Salt fell overboard!
"Woman overboard!" shouted Mrs. Salt.
Sally Salt came to the rescue.
But still the *Jolly Jack* tipped up
and down—and Sally Salt fell overboard, too!
"Girl overboard!" shouted Sally Salt.

The next minute surprising things happened.
Somebody threw a rope to Mr. Salt.
  "That's clever!" said Mr. Salt.
Somebody threw a life ring to Mrs. Salt.
  "Just what I need!" Mrs. Salt said.
Somebody threw a rubber tube
to Sally Salt. She did not say a word.
  Somebody had rescued them all!

"What a surprise!" said Mrs. Salt.
"Look who it is!" said Mr. Salt.
"It's Sammy!" said Sally.
   Sammy Salt made hot drinks
for his family.
He wrapped them up in blankets.
He steered the ship.

"Now I know who tickled my nose,"
said Mr. Salt.
   "And drank my cocoa," said Sally Salt.
   "And ate my boiled egg!" Mrs. Salt said.
   "That's right," said Sammy Salt. "It was me!"

After that the best things happened.
The storm blew away.
The *Jolly Jack* reached
Coconut Island.

Mr. and Mrs. Salt prepared a picnic
on the shore.

Sally and Sammy played hide-and-seek
in the jungle.

Bedtime came.
Mr. and Mrs. Salt and the children
slept out under the stars.
   Then, during the night,
the last thing happened.
Sammy Salt woke up.
   "My nose keeps tickling," he said.

The End